I0626169

Obliterated: Everything is About To Change

Chris Mentillo

Published by Horror Press Publishing, 2018.

While every precaution has been taken in the preparation of this book, the publisher assumes no responsibility for errors or omissions, or for damages resulting from the use of the information contained herein.

OBLITERATED: EVERYTHING IS ABOUT TO CHANGE

First edition. July 2, 2018.

ISBN: 978-0692753286

Written by Chris Mentillo.

Also by Chris Mentillo

Obliterated: Everything is About To Change

Watch for more at https://HorrorPublishing.com.

Table of Contents

For my beautiful Wife Gloria. You mean the world to me.

For my beautiful wife, Gloria. Thank you for putting up with me for all these years. Hope it pays off one day. You mean the world to me.

Works by Chris Mentillo

Other published books, songs, and scripts written by, Chris Mentillo on horror, music, true-crime, fiction, nonfiction, the paranormal, macabre, and supernatural horror:

Books:

"The Adventures of Little Eugene."
(Scary, Children Poems)
"Infinite Abundance."
(Spirituality)
"A True Tale of Horror." The Unhappy Heiress
(Classic Horror Series).
(Horror, Paranormal, Supernatural)
"Weird Tales of Horror." Stories from the Dead
(Classic Horror Series).
(Horror, Paranormal, Supernatural)

Film & Music:

"THE WITCH BOARD PROJECT"
"All Alone Again"
"Broken Heart"
"Charles Manson: End of Days"
"Pretty Girl"
"Cheating"
"Fool of Hearts"
"I'm heading for the Train"
"Rocking Roll Santa"
"She's Gonna Kill Me"
"Staring"
"We like It Quiet"
"Yesterday, Today, and Tomorrow The Beatles"
"Woods Stalker"
"Monster Attack"

"It was a bright white light. We followed it to Bakersfield, and all of a sudden, to our utter amazement, it went straight up in the heavens. When I got off the plane I told Nancy about it."

Ronald Reagan, describing his 1974 UFO sighting.

Introduction:

"Imagine the perfect domicile where there is little if any crime, a safe haven jam-packed with welcoming neighbors, a profusion of popular sports to partake in, plenty of stimulating recreational activities everyone can enjoy, white picket fences, pristine lakes, lush greenery, and gorgeous mansions — the ideal kind-of-home to raise your kids in even.

Now picture this same sanctuary where come hell or high water, when the sun subsides, something causes everyone and everything to turn 360 degrees out of control — a place where teenagers and adults are possessed with becoming widespread or even famous for becoming one of the residence lifeguards. What is instigating these things to happen? Why are people missing and acting so outlandish? Why can no one remember?

There is one tenacious, single-minded lifeguard however, who is painstakingly persistent to find out, but has no idea of the physical and mental anguish she will endure while trying to unravel the mystery behind this nightmare."

I encompassed the books synopsis into the introduction above, to remind you again of the stories plot, and to receptively help set the atmosphere. I truly hope you will enjoy this book. The story becomes progressively exciting. Think of all the scary stories you have heard of, scene or read before in your lifetime — stories of the macabre, terrifying malformed monsters, unidentified creatures, and spine-chilling looking aliens from places, not of this world. I assume you have a keen interest in this, otherwise, you probably would not be reading this right now. Better yet, perhaps you even had your own personal experience with the paranormal and supernatural. Most of my books evolve around these themes, because I have had more than my own fair share of experiences with the supernatural, etc.

I never did presume to become a horror writer, but plagued by innumerable ghastly nightmares, and daunting endless, and sleep deprived nights, I began writing my dreams down. I have over one thousand or more pages of squirmy nightmares written down in my journals. Many zealous readers began to first shadow me through such stories told on my radio show. From there, everything first evolved, and well... as they say, "the rest is history."

I would like to first start by saying; every non-fiction or fiction book should have an introduction. The prologue or introduction of any book can help both the author and reader better bond with one another. The goal here then, is to establish a true connection between the two of us — by helping you appreciate a little more about this book, and about myself.

A golden rule of thumb (when writing any book) is, "never assume you know something or someone too well." That being said, lets first start off by getting to know the book better, and address the book's title, *"Obliterated."* What does it all mean? Well there are several elucidations and delineations for the title of this book, "Obliterated." Therefore, I have taken the liberty of defining the word, which I believe, helps best describe, outline, and define what the story is truly about:

I know a good introduction usually prohibits, and therefore omits explaining characterizations, but I really feel the need to elaborate more involving the meaning of the title of this horror book.

"Obliterated," in this sense of this story, simply means *to remove completely from recognition or memory; "efface the memory of the time in the camps" mystify — make mysterious; "mystify the story, to be wiped-out of one's memory completely."*

When we refer to *"obliterate"* in these expressions, we are principally placing all the emphasis on the human mind - the brain. The brain is an intricate one, and does not usually come with a "user friendly manual," does it? Which is one of the reasons why such a book should deliver a well-dressed prelude.

I also inscribed the introduction to this book, to sanguinely explain to you, "what this book isn't about," especially for all my ever-so-wonderful, assuring fans of my preceding-mentioned published books. I am assuming I have some (fans) due to the admiration of my books sales. I mean, just because I have not time-honored all my royalties yet, does not mean I have no, "interested contributing readers." "Not to boast, but I've worked tremendously hard in trying to build a widespread audience of, fascinated readers — especially on the Internet, via my social media grid — something for which I'm enormously delighted about today. Well...I am anyways.

Moreover, if you have had the good fortune of construing any of my previous fictional works of Classic Horror literature, than you undoubtedly — by this time have an indication of the kind of stories I like. Many of these such stories have weird and perverse plots involving the macabre, for which are inundated with individuals and events from centuries ago. For instance, the late 1800's, or the year 1888 has always captivated me. However, this story is a little different because, the style of writing may first appear more like a journal, and the plot of the story exposes true events around the year, 1984.

I have always been riveted with places like Whitechapel in London, England involving the famous, but dubious, 1888 unresolved case of my personal all-time favorite, "Jack the Ripper." In addition, after hours of research reading a seemingly interminable amount of books concerning this baffling mystery, I should however, undeniably accrue at least some credit for identifying myself, a true "Ripperologist." Yes indeed, Jack the Ripper is only one classic example of the many stories for which have captured my attention.

For as long as I can remember, I have speculated in curiosity about the unidentified, and the possible psychological characteristic of why people do what they do. For example, starting with childhood — horror movies, the paranormal, the supernatural, true crime, science fiction, serial killers, mystery books, and freighting horror movies have always intrigued me while growing up as a kid.

Stories, written by Rod Serling's, "The Twilight Zone," series, Alfred Hitchcock's movies, "The Birds," H.P. Lovecraft writings, Edgar Allan Poe's stories, and personal all-time favorite, "Stephen King." These notable horror writers became — recognized for their outstanding contribution to horror literature for a reason. Their stories ordinarily leave some kind of memorable or enduring emotional impact to their audience, and readers.

A true testament to this fact is, how I will never forget when I first watched Stephen Spielberg's movie, "Jaws," and how emotionally distraught I remember it left me. Honestly, my friends and I did not want to venture out swimming for over a year after watching this horror flick. Many other viewers felt the same way — no, wonder why "Stephen Spielberg," is still considered being one of the best in the business.

These are the kinds of emotions very few, but every creative director, actor, producer, artist, musician, and writer should try to attempt to display to their audience — easier said than done — especially with a book. Sometimes you need to go the extra mile, by spending many hard years of steadfast-committed work in order to create, write, develop, produce, and cavalcade such an unadulterated masterpiece. They are not typically made overnight.

The legendary author, "Truman Capote" best exhibits this truth in the development of his book, "In Cold Blood." Capote learned of the quadruple murder, and decided to travel to Kansas and write about the crime. Accompanied by his childhood friend and fellow author — Harper Lee, both writers interviewed local residents and investigators assigned to the case, and took thousands of pages of notes.

The killers, Richard "Dick" Hickock and Perry Smith, were both arrested six weeks after the murders, and Capote initially spent six years working on the book. (Yes you heard correctly — six freaking year-o-ski's). Parts of the book, including important details — differ from actual real events. The book is the second biggest selling true crime book in publishing history, behind author, "Vincent Bugliosi's" 1974 book, "Helter Skelter" (another one of my personal favorites) on the Manson murders.

Can you imagine? It took Capote more than six years to finish this classic masterpiece. To date, his book is perhaps one of the best book's I have ever read on "true crime." Incidentally, his book left me so frightened; I stood up most nights shaking in utter fear, and with all the lights on. In fact, insane as this may sound, I did not sleep for almost a week.

The same may also hold true of Truman Capote himself; many colleagues professed he never transcribed or even endeavored to write another novel after In Cold Blood." Why didn't he write another one? No one really seemed to know why. Perhaps only Capote himself knows the palpable answer to this question.

Not long after the success of his novel, Truman became indisposed, depressed, and reclusive. Perhaps the very "crux" of his own brilliant work took its toll on him. One thing is for sure though; Truman Capote would never be the same after the success of his, chef-d'oeuvre novel, "In cold Blood."

The old adage, "they don't make them like they use too," still holds true today. Nothing beats good old classic horrors like, Bram Stoker's "Dracula," and other notable movies such as "Frankenstein," and "The Mummy," etc. These movies and others have always peeked many "horror fans" interest for years — from all across the globe.

What is it about these individuals and stories which captures the responsiveness, and hearts of so many people? — This question, along with a whirlwind of others, besieged my brain for a long time — even during the creation of this book. Although the story, "Obliterated" is a rather diminutive one; I wanted this precise story to leave the audience psychologically marveling with what really happened by the end of the story, so as to leave you (the reader) pondering with varies emotional challenging thoughts.

Originally, when I first started to pen this novella, I was shooting for a 12,000 word short for a magazine submission. And one of the periodical's publishing submission requirements was to try and leave enough room at the end of the story to possibly be able to crack the story into a full-pledged novel.

So being adamant about submitting such literature (at the time anyway) to this horror magazine, I started to move headfirst in hopes of landing a "publishing contract" with the magazine company. Suffice to say, I never submitted the final draft, (polished copy) and so regrettably the manuscript found its way back to amassing up more space on my computer. A year had passed, and before long, (embarrassingly) two more years came to an abrupt end, before I finally took the initiative to take another hard look at where this story was actually going, and believe me, I still had no clue.

Insane as this sounds, not knowing this tapped the hell out of me. You see, I always have the "mad," ill-fated habit of trying to finish writing books as soon as possible. Call this inpatient, lethargic, negligent, reckless, immoral, or whatever you see fit. However, the truth is, I have always been plagued of nightmares involving dying — before ever being able to finish publishing a book. Therefore, you can imagine how exasperated this made me. I would say to my wife, Gloria (a perfectionist) something like, "God I can't stand it. I have to finish this book by tomorrow – no excuses!" My wife then would reply saying, "Why?" "Don't you want your book to be the very best?" "My usual response to this was all but too routine, and I always responded by saying, "Of course I do, but what if I die tomorrow?" Gloria would always finish having the last word by saying, "Oh God, here we go again."

Lastly, after listening to "All Along the Watchtower," by Mr. Jimmi Hendrix, along with being restless in rigid thought, I decided to give the book a final thwack. I wrote the book as things came into my head — having no specific strategy of development or framework of plot, etc. By doing so, (taking Stephen King's advice) the objective was to try to captivate the reader by not giving away too much facet, of what materializes next throughout the story.

Furthermore, I painstakingly writhed with the likelihood of deciding on which specific genre the story would best be classified as, and if the book should be branded fiction or non-fiction.

I do not want to wiseacre you to tears by explaining how many times I changed the title of this story either. One reason for this indecision was because, a good percentage of the book's story, encompassed actual true events.

If you really think about it, many "awe-inspiring" fiction stories are, based on true-life events. Not to get too much off the main topic here by jumping into, "Writing 101," but yes, most made-up stories (good ones anyways) seem to somehow evolve around or develop from some kind of real-life incident. The writer, "Stephen King" walks his talk by depicting this example quite brilliantly with most of his books. Do you agree?

One other final note I wish to address, is the subject of, "unidentified creatures." These monsters are ordinarily demarcated (by a professional Cryptologist) as being, *big foot, lock ness monster, werewolves, vampires, little silver people, men in black, flying saucers, lizard man, the moth man, ghosts, devils, deities, paranormal and supernatural entities, aliens, alien abductions*, or anything we are not normally used to seeing — "seeing is believing," wouldn't you agree? It was for me.

Many researchers remain incredulous today, due to the insufficient amount of scientific evidence pertaining to these creatures. If anything, attaining more than just a foretaste of one of the above-mentioned creatures will indeed augment a pintsized more believability to even the most skeptical of scientists. Although, finding somewhat of any skeleton remains will substantiate even more credibility.

How about all the misidentifications many individuals' may have in witnessing these unusual proceedings or things? Perhaps they really are erroneously identifying them. Nonetheless, I only believe this to be moderately true. Sure, it is conceivable that some people are too unnerved in the, "spur of the moment," which can lead to panic, and later to a misidentification. However, what about a credible witness boasting a scientific background, or even a professional woodsman, tracker or hunters, who have claimed to see them, and even go as far as passing lie detector tests with, flying colors? They cannot all be, wide of the mark — can they?

Suffice to say, I know this much is true; we live in a vast — untamed world where most anything can easily go undetected. So, is it too hard then for us to emanate an agreement, that there are things, for which none of us knows about out there? I highly think so. Consequently, as a result, we should feasibly have a more open mind about such possibilities.

How about there being a bourgeoning potential for some of these disconcerting and unearthing detections to be of conjectural, unworldly, and supernatural qualities, or paranormal entities of some third world dimension — not from this interval or planet?

One thing is for sure, there is good and evil amongst us here in the world, and we do not have all the answers. None of us is getting out of this planet alive. Eventually, we will wither away into dust, ashes, and skeletons, to one day receive an appropriate entombment. Perhaps only then, will we truly know and have — all the answers to our questions.

July 2015
Boston, Massachusetts

Notable abduction claims:

1956: Elizabeth Klarer (South Africa)
1957: Antonio Vilas Boas (Brazil)
1961: Betty and Barney Hill abduction (USA)]
1973: Pascagoula Abduction (USA)
1975: Travis Walton (USA)
1976: Allagash Abductions (USA)
1978: Valentich disappearance (Australia)
1979: Robert Taylor incident (Scotland)
1970s–1980s: Whitley Strieber (USA)
1990: Danielle Egnew (USA)
1994: Meng Zhaoguo incident (China)
1997: Kirsan Ilyumzhinov (Russia)

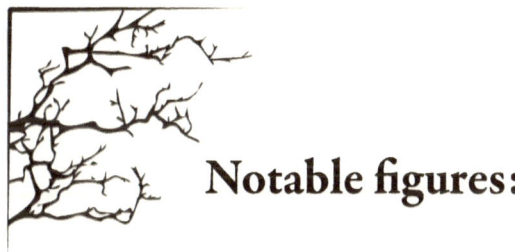

Notable figures:

Brigitte Barclay
     Danielle Egnew
Budd Hopkins
Linda Moulton Howe
David Icke
David M. Jacobs
John E. Mack
Riley Martin
Whitley Strieber

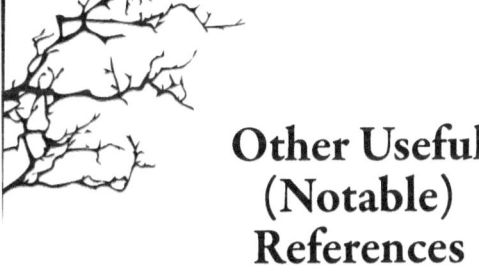

Other Useful
(Notable)
References

ʌ Cuddon, J.A. (1984). Intro: The Penguin Book of Horror Stories. Harmondsworth: Penguin. p. 11. ISBN 0-14-006799-X.

ʌ Rosemary Jackson (1981). Fantasy: The Literature of Subversion. London: Methuen. pp. 53–5, 68–9.

ʌ Richard Davenport-Hines (1998). Gothic: 1500 Years of Excess, Horror, Evil and Ruin. London: Fourth Estate.

ʌ Christopher Frayling (1996). Nightmare: The Birth of Horror. London: BBC Books.

ʌ Brian Stableford, "Robbins, Tod", in David Pringle, ed., St. James Guide to Horror, Ghost & Gothic Writers (London: St. James Press, 1998) ISBN 1558622063 (pp. 480-1).

ʌ Lee Server. Encyclopedia of Pulp Fiction Writers. New York: Facts on File, 2002. ISBN 978-0-8160-4578-5 (pp. 223-224).

ʌ Robert Weinberg, "Weird Tales" in M.B Tymn and Mike Ashley, Science Fiction, Fantasy, and Weird Fiction Magazines. Westport, CT: Greenwood, 1985.ISBN 0-313-21221-X (pp. 727-736).

^ "Unknown". in: M.B. Tymn and Mike Ashley, Science Fiction, Fantasy, and Weird Fiction Magazines. Westport: Greenwood, 1985. pp.694-698. ISBN 0-313-21221-X

^ Richard Bleiler, "Stephen King" in: Bleiler, Ed. Supernatural Fiction Writers: Contemporary Fantasy and Horror. New York: Thomson/Gale, 2003, ISBN 9780684312507. (pp. 525-540).

^ Hillel Italie (September 18, 2003). "Stephen King receives honorary National Book Award". Ellensburg Daily Record. Retrieved 2010-09-12. Stephen King, brand-name writer, master of the horror story and e-book pioneer, has received an unexpected literary honor: a National Book Award for lifetime achievement.

^ K.A. Laity "Clive Barker" in Richard Bleiler, ed. Supernatural Fiction Writers: Contemporary Fantasy and Horror. New York: Thomson/Gale, 2003. ISBN 9780684312507 (pp. 61-70).

^ K.A. Laity, "Ramsey Campbell", in Richard Bleiler, ed. Supernatural Fiction Writers: Contemporary Fantasy and Horror. New York: Thomson/Gale, 2003. ISBN 9780684312507 (pp. 177-188.)

^ "Golden Proverbs". Retrieved 2012-12-15.

^ "Elements of Aversion". Retrieved 2012-11-02.

^ A b Stephanie Demetrakopoulos (Autumn 1977). "Feminism, Sex Role Exchanges, and Other Subliminal Fantasies in Bram Stoker's "Dracula"". Frontiers: A Journal of Women Studies (University of Nebraska Press) 2 (3): 104–113. JSTOR 3346355.

^ "Annotated Bibliography, Dracula". Retrieved 2012-11-02.

^ "Technologies of Monstrosity". Retrieved 2012-11-02.

^ "Lecture Notes for Dracula". Retrieved 2012-11-02.

^ "Elements of Horror". Redlodge. Retrieved 2012-11-02.

^ Anne Radcliffe, "On the Supernatural in Poetry", The New Monthly Magazine 7 (1826): 145–52.

^ Devandra Varma, The Gothic Flame (New York: Russell & Russell, 1966.

^ S.L. Varnado, "The Idea of the Numinous in Gothic Literature," in The Gothic Imagination, ed. G.R. Thompson (Pullman: Washington State University Press, 1974).

^ "The Bram Stoker Awards". Horror Writer's Association. Retrieved 13 April 2010.

^ "IHG Award Recipients 1994-2006". HorrorAward.org. Retrieved October 30, 2014.

^ "IHG Award Recipients 2007". HorrorAward.org. Retrieved October 30, 2014.

^ Brian Stableford, "Horror", in The A to Z of Fantasy Literature, (p. 204), Scarecrow Press, Plymouth. 2005. ISBN 0-8108-6829-6

^ Brian Stableford, "The Discovery of Secondary Worlds: Some Notes on the Aesthetics and Methodology of Heterocosmic Creativity", in Heterocosms. Wildside Press LLC, 2007 ISBN 0809519070 (p. 200).

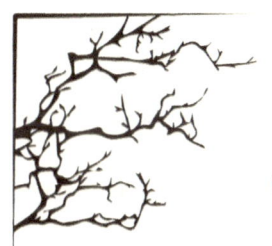

Chapter 1

I laid half asleep in bed, and could not stop the sweat from dripping down my body. The cabins air conditioner broke, and the several ceiling fans in the bedroom did little justice in helping me breath.

I continued to toss and turn all night. Already wide-awake, I grabbed a pack of cigarettes and proceeded outdoors to the front porch. The short time outside gave me only temporary relief from inside my hot enclosed cabin, nestled deep within the woods in Skaneateles, New York.

Directly behind my cabin here in Skaneateles, was considered to be one of the state's most popular lake's. Notorious for being exceptionally clean, the lake's presence gave people the widely held impression you were off somewhere living on a tropical island in the Caribbean.

The water was so amazing, and on some days appeared to be a beautiful dark blue. On other occasions, when the sun's rays beamed down on the lake, the water sported a pristine turquoise color — not the kind of place you consider creepy or terrifying. This, "picture-perfect scene" changed after the sun subsided and evening came. Then it was a different story. The townspeople rarely if ever went out during the nighttime. Somehow, they knew better.

Celebrities from all across the country traveled far to visit this tourist attraction, and shortly thereafter, it did not take them very long to be bitten by what I call, "the village bug." In fact, many who stayed here found complete refuge — so much so, several of them would later find themselves purchasing million dollar summer home mansions, somewhere far out on the water. After living here for a short time though, they would leave town, and for reasons unknown — never come back.

On many occasions I enjoyed taking long drives down, "west-side road," just so I could get a quick glimpse of these beautiful estates owned by, "the rich and famous." At other times, I drove up towards the east end of the village along the lakeside to check out the real huge mansions. Bored with nothing to do, I would park my vehicle on the side of the road to stare, and stare some more. Yet, for some strange reason, I always made sure to leave this area before dark.

Many of the residents living here treasured playing hockey, and If you did not play or somehow become involved, you were not considered to be a true village resident. The same thing stood with most of the recreational water sports—mainly consisting of snorkeling, waterskiing, and swimming.

Of course, if you are one of the lucky ones who owned a piece of property with access to your very own private waterfront, you did not have the burden of having to use the public beach to do these activities. Instead, you had all the clandestineness you wanted, and the sovereignty to do as you wished. Most residents would rather avoid using public areas of the lake for this reason. Unfortunately, though, some (not so stable lifeguards who always took their job too serious) patrolled these areas. They never let their guard down, and you would never see them walking around, mingling and philandering with other people.

These lifesavers never let their safeguard down period. Many of them were in top shape, and usually fortified themselves with what I call, "lifeguard ammunition." Whatever apparatus they needed in order to save an impending drowning or injured person, these guys carried it everywhere they went, even during their break time and when using the lavatory.

Yep, they were excessively serious, and many people living in the village often interrogated their outlandish behavior. This has not always been the case though. Notwithstanding, plenty of folks around town began conjecturing if some sort of overpowering freestanding force was to blame.

One lifeguard in particular, who I will call "Bulldog," the more somber of the cluster, had what girls would consider, (and maybe other guys too) "a killer body," but sported a freighting face of an attack dog. His facial expressions lived up to his nickname and only intensified when he blew one of his several whistles, which he carried securely latched around his neck.

They came in all various shapes, sizes, and colors. One whistle was red, engraved with a Red Cross emblem, (the bigger one) a blue medium sized one, and a yellow one, which appeared a bit eroded — perhaps from the privation of use or from getting too wet. I always saw him expending his big red whistle. When Bulldog blew his whistle, man did it ever give off a god-forsaken loud pitch sound. This is his most treasured one, and by far his brassiest. I rarely if ever-recalled Bulldog blustering into his blue whistle, and I never saw him reach out for his yellow whistle. I still do not know why he always carried three of them. Nevertheless, the point is he is obvious by far the most serious lifeguard on the lake. Guess you just have to respect someone like this.

One day Bulldog had his dream come true when he became, "managing supervisor," placed in charge of other lifeguards. This new position also consisted of training all those other "poor individuals" who wanted to get their lifeguard certification. I guess they thought Bulldog made a great candidate for this, maybe because they figured he would make it more challenging for other new lifeguards to obtain their merit badges, or for those needing to maintain their lifeguard prominence. God help them all!

The lucky guards, (who showed promising athletic ability in receiving their certification), were considered heroes. You see, when you worked on the lake as a lifeguard, people treated you like royalty. Honestly, the best thing you could be in town was a "certified lifeguard." So as a result, you were considered… well, one of the more ubiquitous ones living in the village. Everyone, including all the other teenagers looked up to you as some kind of celebrity. However, the only problem with obtaining this whole lifeguard fecund is how expensive it was to become certified. In addition, certification is exceptionally hard to complete, since Bulldog became, "the new-head trainer." By the following year however, this would all change.

The local Y.M.C.A, who sponsored the lifeguard certification, only employed the best — fit guards. They could do this because their amount of supply, far suppressed their demand. Everyone, including their own mother wanted to be a lifeguard on the lake, and for recognizable reasons. Even older folks would give this a whack.

Hell, one year an eighty-year old woman once tried out for certification. One of her dreams had been to one day become a guard. Older people applauded her on, but she still had not conjured up enough nerve to give her lifelong dream a shot.

One day she decided to try out, and though she never made the cut, she did however became the talk of the village. She even had her picture plastered all over the front page of several local correspondents, including an inspirational article written up about her experience. Unfortunately, though, shortly after the "Daily Penny Saver" published her story, she went missing. Until this day, no one had ever seen or heard from her again. She was not the only person to disappear involving lifeguards while pursuing their certification. Many other (whom I will refer to as, "unfortunates") would soon join her.

Plain and simple, the towns' people were jubilant about the whole lifeguard bonanza. Every year, newer, younger, and more serious lifeguards, supplanted the older burnt out ones — if any were still around.

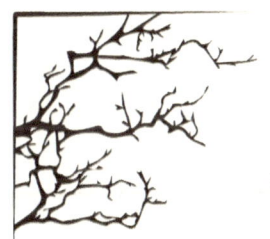

Chapter 2

I am not quite sure how this all transpired. What I do hark back to though is a lot of tossing and turning in bed. Something deliberately began to woe me. I refused to believe the heat was the culprit for keeping me wide-awake. Instead, I realized deep down inside, something else (maybe even sinister) was brewing in the air!

I do not label myself as a psychic, however I do have a rather keen sense of predication. These so-called predictions usually came in the form of a dream, but this was much different. This night, I did not even get a twinkle of sleep. Something kept me up all night — peaking my interest. This mystified me, and provoked my curiosity. What is this, which came over me? Did I feel good things, or perhaps far worse and sinister? I stood on the cabin porch-smoking cigarette after cigarette, pondering on those thoughts while I continued to gawp off — out into the webbed foggy water.

I had not comprehended it yet, but many of the bizarre chain of events began on this night, starting first when I could hear a high-pitched noise resonance out from the lake. The sound had been an all too acquainted one, and I rumored to myself, am I envisaging this? What is all this ringing in the ears about? Am I in a daze — half-asleep, and sleepwalking? Then I started to think, is this another psychotic dream?

I had the lights off to smoke in amity and seepage the hundreds of moths, which endlessly tried to cleave onto the porch lights. With no streetlights on, the scene outdoors now became an eerie one.

The cabin I lived in, is not only surrounded by a primeval lake, but is nestled deep inside the woods. Little if any people are nearby, and I mounted there sheltered from cultivation and unaccompanied in the dark.

I am all by myself out here in the middle of nowhere, gazing off out into the lake, when an earsplitting noise reverberated out again which continued to echo into my ear. Then, without caveat, something caught the viewpoint of my eye. A flash of impenetrable, black smoke soared by. This thing winged by so fast; I did not get a respectable foretaste — only an abrupt gloomy shadow, conceded by which appeared to be some kind of condensation. It was pitch black out, and somehow this peculiar manifestation became visible to the stark-naked eye.

Seconds later, a cold winter chill hit me like a ton of bricks — hot and humid outside one minute, to feeling as though I had walked into a freezer the next. The little voice inside, prompted me this was not good. I could not help imagine what could happen next. Instincts told me to head for safety, but my curiosity as usual got the best of me. Like an idiot out of some horror movie, I stood motionless trying to rationalize to myself what had happened.

I began to conjure up some lame — rash excuse for this unusual activity. Then, not more than a few seconds later, a well-lit light blinded me. Bam... Bam, the robust beam went on and off, and became so blinding, that after finally fading away, I still could not see.

Not long after regaining eye site, I scanned the premise — searching for the basis from where the light came from. I could not find a damn thing. As I slowly turned my head out toward the lake, I suddenly realized... I was now no longer alone; And out there standing in the distance, appeared to be a dark shadowy figure.

I stood shivering, and ice-covered in disbelief. I have never seen anything like this before, and had no idea what it was. I strained my eyes to get a better view, but everything looked vague. This rare daunting looking thing appeared covered with a black veneer. No legs, no arms, only a sketch of a shadowy entity with a large head, which showed little evidence of having any eyes, or even a anthropological looking face.

Minutes passed by, and the strange tall slender dark figure in the distance still had not nudged. What does this thing want? Why does he not move? Why is it gawking at me? The whole experience creeped me out, leaving me terrified, and frozen scared out of my wits.

"Hello... Who the hell are you... what do you want?" I shouted. The stranger had no reply.

The eccentric image began to move toward the porch, and my heart sank into my stomach. This thing slowly inched closer in my direction. Seconds later, I heard strange moans, and clatters, but I could not make out what this thing was implying. The voice sounded almost Latin — emulating a very unusual kind of alien dialect — not from this earth. Was it trying to communicate?

I had not detected this character's face, and without warning, the thing stopped and turned its head to the lake. Moments later, an arm appeared into the picture, and a long skeleton like finger began to point out towards the water (kind of reminded me of those fingers from the creature in the television show, "Tales from The Crypt." It kept his arm and one finger pointed out, and the head swiveled back and forth and then back into place.

Now staring, another hand came into view, which appeared to be holding something. The strange being or entity elevated its arm, and then that all too conversant high-pitched sound rang out again — piercing into my ear. This time however, it seemed much louder — becoming almost unbearable.

Before long, I found myself on the ground casing both ears with my hands. I screamed at the top of my lungs for the sound to sojourn. I thought I was going to die. After the noise stopped, I grabbed my porch-wooded railing to pull myself up. I turned my responsiveness towards the figure, and the thing tilted his head to the left, slightly to the right, and vanished.

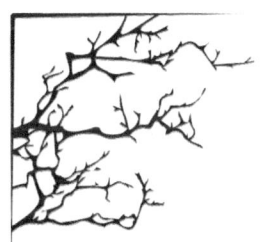

Chapter 3

I am not sure how I ended up here, but I did. I found myself in my bedroom, lying on my back, and staring at the cabin ceiling. I had not remembered anything much, only bits and portions of being outside, a strange noise, and nothing else. I glanced over for a time check. Anomalous I thought; My watch specified more than four hours had elapsed from the first time I last left the room to smoke, and return back to the bedroom. Skeptical, I poked the Rolex a couple more times with my index finger, and quavered the watch back and forth to double check. Yep! Sure enough, somehow I could not account for those four missing hours. I tried to recall what happened,

but everything was still a blur. A few minutes more passed by,

until I finally closed my eyes and fell asleep.

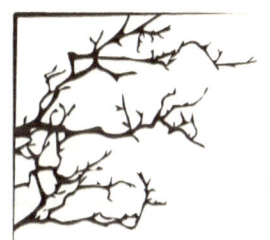

Chapter 4

By morning time, I found myself preparing to meet with a friend at the local donut shop. I did not have to worry about being late, seeing my only trepidations would be nothing except for lakes, farms, and cornfields. I was not certain why I needed to meet with him, but I did.

Upon arrival, two folks were quarreling with one another. One of these men (looked to be about in his late forties) tried to coax the other one to go into his vehicle. The other man counterattacked, and soon a boxing match broke out between the two. I began to intervene until a State Trooper spotted the fight. The troopers name is Hank Freely.

Before becoming a trooper, he worked as a decorated New York City police officer, who experienced his first bought of law enforcement work as a patrol officer in the pugnacious streets of the Bronx. A handsome, but hard-hitting burly Irishman of half-Hungarian Jewish descent, Hank had seen everything. He went through all of the shit regarding the twin tower bombings, and almost died three times for being in several gunfight battles. What is most astounding about him is his age. Hank is only twenty-five years old, but by looking at him, one may assume he looked at least forty.

Despite his prolific reputation as a decorated cop, along with his spectacular handsome features, Freely's heavy drinking, beginning from his teenage days would soon get the best of him. His obsessive binges tiptoed up on him, and when not seen driving his patrol car around the village or lake, you found him out many nights hitting-up the local hick bars. He was not married, and had no children (that he and others in town knew of), and he never spoke much. Hank stayed quiet regarding most of his personal life, (which was never free of tumult), and always kept his difficulties to himself.

One night, after a heavy drinking splurge with a few local cops, he went on a rampage. (Freely's excessive consumption of alcohol, and frequent dating games would undeniably come back to rendezvous with him).

The story goes... one of the girls he wooed happened to be married. She had been the wife of a retired State Police Corporal. She was much younger than her husband was (by almost twenty years), and who like Freely, also had an unruly drinking problem. To the townspeople, she had a repute for being a home wrecker and police groupie. A petite — attractive looking girl, she stood around "5" feet tall.

Anecdotes spread in town, that on most weekends she was screwing around with Hank in his cruiser. These stories — were only speculations at the time, and nothing seemed to come of them. However, that all changed on one "hot sweaty" weekend, during July 4.

According to the village people, Hank Freely and her were spotted together drinking outside, "The Lake Lodge." Both appeared to be tanked-up. A quarrel began, and a fight pursued.

The following morning, she never came home and was reported missing. The only trace of evidence indicating her being out this night on the 4th happened to be when a pair of panties showed up, which the authorities later officially identified as belonging to her.

One witness did come forward, asserting he thought he speckled her walking along near a popular trail with an unknown stranger — not far from the local town's donut shop. Three days later, the FBI came into town to query Hank Freely and the Corporal (her husband).

After an extensive investigation, both of the men were no longer primary suspects regarding her disappearance. Nonetheless, the damage was done with the whole ordeal, and subsequently Hank's vaunted reputation in town became somewhat tarnished. Consequently, many people would have their doubts regarding ever trusting him again. Later on, they suspended him for one month without pay, pending an internal investigation.

Ever since then, not much transpired concerning Freely, the girl, and the incident. In fact, everything had remained unobtrusive in the village, until this tiff between both men outside the donut shop. Now while gazing closer at them arguing, I realized I recognized them.

The shorter man was retired police Corporal, "David Zimmerman." Zimmerman is married to the women who Hank Freely dated. She is also the person reported missing. The other man — the taller of the two men, is "Billy B. Carter," known by others as, "old man farmer Bill."

Billy stood some "6 feet 10," weighing in at a bulky 300 plus pounds. Not someone you want to pick a fight with, and not your run-of-the-mill type person.

Bill bears a resemblance to the famous French wrestler, "Andrey the Giant.' Nonetheless, He may be half Bill's size, but Zimmerman could hold his own. However, the Corporal's aforementioned notability as a championship kick-boxer gave credence to his untarnished reputation as a mean street fighter, and he displayed no signs of backing down from this fight.

Unexpectedly, Hank jumped in between both men, and tried to stop them from killing one another.

"Mind your own damn business Freely you murdering, rotten, crummy, no good for nothing home wrecker," shouted Corporal Zimmerman.

"Easy there Corporal, you don't want to humiliate yourself by being placed in handcuffs while being sent to the county jail — do you Corporal?" replied Freely!

"Alright...please, both of you, pipe down already and tell me what the ruckus is about," stated Freely.

I am not going to speak to you, shouted Zimmerman. The Corporal continued...

"No offense, but you make me nauseas just by looking at you, and you're going to get what's coming to you too... You'll see... you can count on it."

Hank Freely snarled at Zimmerman, then the Corporal got into his car peeling out — kicking back dirt and dust onto both men.

Corporal Zimmerman sped off, slammed on his breaks, rolled down his window, looked at Bill and yelled out..."I'm not thru with you either, you big fat smelly, imprudent pig." Seconds later Zimmerman gunned it, and drove off down the potholed street.

Freely shivered his head, turned to old man farmer Bill and probed him for additional material. While he stood listening to Bill, he scribbled down imperative notes onto his Police logbook.

Upon further interviewing Billy, Freely continued to question him, regarding why Zimmerman would want to pick a fight with him. Bill explained to him that he was as baffled about Zimmerman's abrasive conduct towards him as he was.

Bill said he was minding his own business, when Zimmerman approached him calling him every obscenity under the sun. Bill continued, and told Freely before he could find out what the fuss was about, Zimmerman sucker punched him. "Then you jumped in to break the fight up," stated Bill.

"I'm a little muddled by all this," muttered Freely, but I'm going to get to the bottom of this, despite what Zimmerman thinks."

Old man farmer Bill looked at him shivering his head and said, "I don't know what's up Zimmerman's ass these days, but for some strange reason this whole damn town is going wacky"

"Sheee, do you hear that?" whispered Freely. "Yes, sure do! Sounds like your police radio," specified Zimmerman.

The two of them stood soundless while listening to Freely's portable cue in, "cuuu, cuuu...trooper Freely, what's your twenty? Get over to the barracks ASAP. There's a bad storm in effect, and it's gonna be a mean one."

"Gotta jet," chirped Freely.

Freely told Bill, (before leaving) to stay away from Zimmerman. He jumped into his cruiser, turned on the auxiliary lights, switched his sirens on, and took off from the donut shop's parking lot — disappearing down the street.

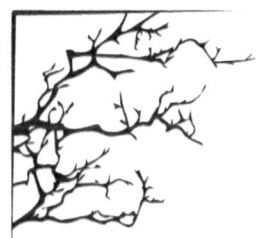

Chapter 5

I began to track old man farmer Bill as he came out of the donut shop after ordering his usual two Boston crème donuts, along with his extra, extra, large coffee. I approached him from behind with my vehicle and continued to shadow him — keeping a remote enough distance away from him.

Bill lived only about two miles past the pet cemetery on a farm up in the hills, which was surrounded by nothing more than, tall cornfields, spooky cranberry apple trees, plenty of wooded trajectories, all breeds of animals (not many humans), and most notably, the town's stunning lake.

I only needed to tail behind him for a minute or two, before he took to the thickets; so I could park my car near the opening of the entryway, which leads straight into a gaunt trail. I waited for a few minutes until I saw him, far-off enough ahead in the brush, then I completed my move, and hastily trailed him from behind.

While I continued to trek through the heavy timbered wilderness, it dawned on me...What am I doing? Why do I feel compelled to track old man farmer Bill anyway?

Am I going insane? Had I grown so bored with my life that I needed to stoop this low? Oh well, nobody's perfect. I giggled at myself for a while, until I shrugged it off.

Moments later, dark black clouds consumed every inch of the sky, causing the sun to fade. Panic set in, and the wind began to pick-up, blowing and stirring up dirt and leaves off the trail, forming miniature tornadoes. From everywhere, large tree limbs and branches fell like rain from far above, and as I continued to follow Bill through the woods, I suddenly had second thoughts of aborting the mission, thinking perhaps I had gone mad or something!

By now, I became a bit nervous, confused, and rather fearful of my own behavior. I thought for a moment of how I wished I were back at the cabin. I could not even recall where old man farmer Bill departed.

To make matters worse, I had not ever seen his home before. His residence was out here tucked away deep in the forest off the trail somewhere hidden. He had trudged these trails to his farmhouse every day, and as far as I knew, he had been the only one fearless enough, or crazy enough to even contemplate walking out here, especially when the sun goes down. Bill was plain batty for living by himself — out in the middle of nowhere, and so far away from civilization.

There were no optical signs of anything — nothing out here, and as I began to think about this awful dreary setting, I precipitously found myself overwhelmed with unsettling feelings, which made me feel more uncomfortable; like all those previous unnerving haunting stories of spiritual existence, ghosts, and aliens. Allegedly, these absurd paranormal beings only came out to life, and linger about throughout the night. Deformed, "short people" with bloody pitchforks, abnormal wrinkled skin, and staggering evil eyes of death, immediately inundated my brain.

Most of the residents living in the village became petrified of old man farmer Bill. By many people's standards, he was nothing more than a "nut and loner." The strange peculiar short people Bill frequently spoke about stood only a couple of feet tall (if that). Bill would often say in a frenzy like manner, "they are not of this world."

Those individuals who mentioned these, "little monsters" while at the donut shop, were always considered by the townspeople as being, "wackos and nut-bags." They also became easy prey for making fun of. Bill is no exception. Bill had not lied about anything in his life, and had never been guilty of nothing other than an occasional little exaggeration from time to time.

Yet despite Bill's outstanding reputation for being candid, some of the people in town began to wonder if Bill really told the truth about these happenings. Folks who are more religious assumed Bill could do no wrong, and believed he would never lie, regarding such things.

Thinking of Bill's stories while walking in the murky woods sent goose thumps over the entire body. To make matters worse, it was now darker than ever, with little signs of Bill anywhere, and the trail appeared to be ending — splitting in two separate directions.

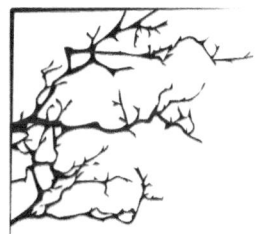

Chapter 6

By now I started to fret, and the panic attacks begin to set in. I could not breathe and before long, I began gasping for air. Nevertheless, I continued to survey the present path, all along second-guessing my choice of directions, and wondering if the verdict to move ahead was the correct one.

I thought for a moment of how I should have backtracked by taking the other trail, which branched off in the opposite direction. In the past, "instincts" always paid off involving such dilemmas, but for some reason, this time I chose to discount them.

Despite all the anxiety, I tried to remain composed, and as I made my way further up the path, I prayed I would spot old man farmer Bill wandering off somewhere in the woodlands. Bill, where are you... where did you go? I said to myself.

With both hands still clutched against the chest, I started to feel exceptionally dizzy, so I decided to halt and take a short breather to catch my breath. Luckily, not too far up ahead I found myself an old tree stump to sit on.

As I sat down to rest, things that go bump in the night started appearing out of everywhere, and my cell phone beeped informing me of an incoming text. Then the strangest thing happened, and the number 999 appeared, followed by a second call. Thank God, I still can get some kind of reception out here. Who is this, I wondered? Habitually I always make a habit to never answer phone calls or texts from people who are not on my call list. However, because of these, "unusual circumstances" I decided to go for it.

"Hello... hello," I muttered. I waited a few more moments and still no voice — no talking, no noise, no one. I pressed the cell phone up against my ear waiting for anything — some kind of retort. A couple seconds later, I heard what sounded like a faint sigh, along with very heavy breathing, and lots of loud static.

"Who the hell is this?" I yelled!

With the cellular still glued to the side of my head, an all too familiar sound blasted out, causing me to drop the phone. The noise was so intense... I clear fell backwards. I continued to fall and fall, for what seemed like eternity. I didn't realize it yet, but on the way down thoughts of being unable to escape "the reality of serious misfortune," soon proved inevitable.

Upon further descending, I could feel unbearable pain penetrate through my body, when razor like sharp branches stemming outward from several trees tore deep into my flesh — tearing me up — vigorously bouncing me around like a rag doll, and then... "Complete utter darkness."

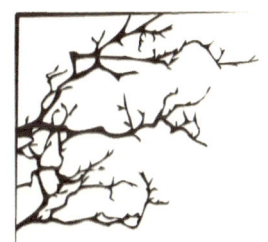

Chapter 7

After I came to, I found myself buried in what appeared to be horse hay. With my eyesight impaired, I tried to lift myself up, when excruciating pain shot up and down my entire body. Now I could feel warm blood dribble down my forehead and down the side of my face, and onto my shirt, which was completely drenched in blood.

Soon visualization became clearer, and I noticed a figure in the far distance, but I was unable to see much... due to it being pitch dark outside.

Bill... that you?" I shouted. Then the strange silhouette Tulsa stood frozen for a moment, and slowly walked away — disappearing into the night.

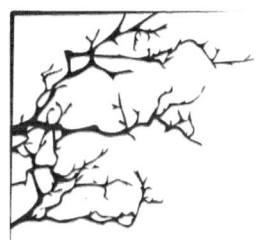

Chapter 8

Afraid, in agony, and once again alone, the immediate impulse (out of fear) was to escape from any further imminent danger, but not before first going for the phone. After all, luck had not been on my side. Shit I thought, I forgot I dropped the damn thing on the way down from the fall. How did I manage to lose what would have been, my main life-line? Could I be any stupider?

After scolding myself for being so careless, I needed out of this mess quickly. I wiped my forehead with my blood soaked shirt, and walked further out into the unknown, anticipating finding some clues of my whereabouts.

Nevertheless, I had not seen any signs of civilization anywhere; people, cars, houses, lakes and streams, or even Bill, who by now became the least of my concern. Something also reminded me of the horror movie, "The Texas Chainsaw Massacre." This gave me the "heavy chivies."

Then, while I continued to focus ahead, something grabbed my attention, and a frigid chill passed through me — catching me off guard. This rather unusual coldness jolted the whole body as if I had been electrocuted by a high dose of electricity. (Once again, I was inundated with more "unfortunate circumstances)." The power of the electrical jolt propelled me sprawling to the ground with such force — sending me airborne midair...landing some twenty feet away.

A few moments later, I tried awkwardly to pull myself up, when suddenly a flickering ray of light shined on my eyes. The beam came from the direction of the dwelling directly in front of me. (This had been identical as the previous one, which blinded me while smoking on my porch the night before).

I raised both hands up over my face to shield its powerful beam from blinding me, but I was too late. Not more than a few seconds later, an overwhelming burning sensation scorched my eyeballs and skull.

Soon the distinct smell of burnt flesh filled the air, as fire began to burn my scalp and eyes — consuming my entire face with red-hot balls of flames. I stood screaming in agony at the top of my lungs, sending an eerie blood-curdling echo out into the darkness. I tried to smother out the blaze, but in doing so my arms caught on fire. Flesh started melting from everywhere.

Now holding my eyes and scalp with both hands (which were literally burning), I panicked and ran for the mysterious dwelling ahead — hoping in some crazy way to soothe the pain. Nevertheless, before I had a chance to reach it, a strong whirl of wind came from behind — sweeping me off my feet. This tremendous supernatural wind-like force stifled out the fire, and for a moment, I encountered a sense of utter solace. Then a strange aura besieged my entire body — forming a long tunnel around me. Almost magically, I was in a complete state of utter bliss and serenity.

Burnt badly, and now entombed inside this blackish funnel — fifty feet or so in front, I saw a bright red colored door. I only noticed it lit up from within the tunnel; everything else appeared entirely dark with no one around me, but myself, the tunnel, and this spine-chilling looking red door. I was rather hesitant while approaching it, but realized I had little... if any choice.

Something supernatural had forced, and pulled me toward this door. I tried hard to walk away in the opposite direction, but the forceful energy had complete control over me, and wrenched me back. Regardless of how much I forced myself to overcome the power of this thing, I became overtaken by the strength of the strong hypnotic force, which continued to drive me straight forward like a magnet in front of this mysterious red phenomenon.

By the time I reached the entrance, I could hear laughing (a high-pitched sinister laugh), that made the hair on my neck, and entire body stand up. Again, this prevailing force continued to tug me through the already opened door — like some sort of haunted house ride.

While inside, in the distance, I observed an obscure stairwell heading in a downward direction. The stairs formed a shape of a figure eight, with each step descending further down. Directly from behind, I felt cold fingers of death rest on my shoulders, and more nudged me from behind the legs

— pushing and guiding me farther down the spiral staircase. It was too dark to realize whose hands were on me, but something beckoned me not to look.

I am beyond petrified at this point, and the bliss and serenity, which consumed me earlier, had longed vanished... while the curiosity of not knowing who remained touching my body made things even worse. Therefore, without hesitating, I decided to quickly turn my head to get a peek, but saw nothing, and they released themselves off my shoulders and legs. I looked back in front of me, and the fingers returned; this time resting on my neck, and soon creeping over my head.

Soon multiple hands began to push me from behind the legs again. I tried a couple more times to catch them in the act, trying to turn back quicker with each attempt, but they were too fast. This strange ordeal became inexplicable.

Upon repeating this procedure, these things continued to return, until I decided to try and move just my eyes. This time I prepared myself. I waited for a few seconds, and quickly rolled only my eyeballs (keeping my entire body stationary) to the side as far as possible.

What followed next is of such cryptic nature that I thought I had been dreaming, and as soon as my eyes moved to the side, there before me were four, slanted glowing red eyes. There were two above my head, and more appeared closely behind my legs. I remained fixated on them, and within seconds, they disappeared.

For a brief moment, the feeling of being touched no longer engrossed my body. Every so often though, I made a habit to glance back — hoping not to discover any more surprises.

Chapter 9

I am not sure why all this happened to me, but as I continued to descend further — spiraling downward in this dark tunnel into the unknown, I began to have a series of intense flashbacks. I was taken back to the beginning of it all — so I thought. First, with me waking up and going out to the porch for a cigarette, to the strange occurrence with the piercing loud noise, to the bright lights, to the black cloudy mist with the creepy slender stranger pointing out towards the lake, to waking up again, and finding myself driving out the next morning to the donut shop. Then followed Freely,

Corporal Zimmerman, and me trailing old man farmer Bill to

the trail — later rendering horrific acts of torture, and now the

tunnel with these unpleasant flashbacks.

I told myself this is one gigantic dream, and I would wake up from all this and laugh this off as another bad nightmare. Moreover, if this is... only one of those horrible dreams, certainly this is as real as they come. Still, none of this made any sense. I wanted this shit to end. I needed to get back to living a normal life — if ever there was such a thing. I wished I never followed old man farmer Bill...

What in the hell was I thinking? What did I want with Bill anyway? Why had I decided to start following him in the first place? Had I gone mad?

Deep down inside I realized there had to be a reason for all this, but I could not recall what this was. I didn't remember anything. Why should I feel this way anyway? Why can't this just go away? I wondered if somehow I was to blame for this!

I began fretting more about many of these occurrences, until I found myself back inside the car, and parked alongside the trail — supposedly leading to, "old man farmer Bill's house." I glanced at my Swiss Army watch and observed much time had passed by. I thought for a moment and tried to recall why I had parked here. I had no memory of what transpired hours before.

I sat for a while, staring out the window at Bill. I continued to stare at him until he disappeared into the woods. As the attention lingered off Bill, I instead focused on the weather. I remembered something regarding Freely talking about a real bad storm, and recalled nothing else.

Moments later, someone approached my car from the rear. It was Trooper Freely. I figured that maybe he came over to warn me of the pursuing squall to come. He parked his vehicle behind mine, got out of his patrol car, and walked over towards me, and asked, "what's ya doing out here all by yourself young lady?" My face turned blush red as I smiled at him and replied, "Um...ah well you see officer, I drove out to this location to kind of relax my mind and ponder on some thoughts. I love the peaceful silence of the woods and all...if you know what I mean?"

As I continued answering Freely, deep down inside I thought about how I had not one damn clue why the hell I'd been out here anyway. I could not remember much — only small bits and pieces. I wondered if he even noticed my face turn red as I answered his questions. I am sure he was not buying any of my story.

After I finished giving him my story, a long pause followed. He stared straight into my eyes, (for what seemed like eternity) smiled at me, and began to laugh. He just stood over me while he continued to let out the most obnoxious sound I ever heard. I tried to restrain myself from laughing at him, but I was too late and found myself unable to hold back any longer, so I broke out with laughter. I could not help myself; this whole ordeal struck me as funny — him chuckling aloud this way. Suddenly he stopped while I remained giggling out of control.

"What do you think I am girl, some kind of stupid turd or something?" He shouted.

"No sir... not at all, I never thought this Sir," I replied.

"You stay put here, and don't move a hair. If you do...I'll be sure to cap some lead into that little cute head of yours girl. You understand... I said you get me young lady?"

I answered Freely back, thinking he had overreacted a bit..."ya I got it."

Soon I started to worry what Hank might do next. I remembered all the people in town mention how ever since the FBI began their investigation into Zimmerman's wife's disappearance, Freely was considered a loose cannon. Regardless, this had not always been the case with him. In the past, he showed positive signs of having a good head on his shoulder. It was as if a freakish black cloud of pure evil held the town, (and some of the town's most reputable people) captive.

Hank was one of the first few townspeople impacted by this. Something took over the old competent trooper from before, and caused him to behave rather strange and very unstable. Reports indicated he beat up lots of individuals for no apparent reason, and not many witnesses came forward to complain. Most of them were in very bad shape and remained hospitalized.

These senseless beatings involving, "innocent victims" always took place out in the middle of nowhere. He never left many clues behind either, and as a result, nobody could say what happened to them but Freely himself. Furthermore, it would be his word over theirs, and even though he began to get a bad rap with the town's people out here, there had never been any substantial concrete proof that he ever did anything wrong; no real evidence — no witnesses either.

Yep, he had been free to do as he wished, and just because the townspeople no longer trusted him, he still was, considered by most... to be a well-respected, former decorated police officer — even amongst his fellow comrades.

Recent reports stated many of the individuals he had suspected of doing things to, had prior arrest records on them. On the other hand though, some of them later checked out fine, and so therefore were considered squeaky clean by many people's standards. Although, not Hank. For some peculiar strange reason, he never saw things this way anymore.

Without a doubt, his behavior struck me as being rather odd, and knowing what I know about Freely, I became intimidated by this, and uncomfortable being in his presence. In the past, I have been pulled over, but I never experienced such unnecessary abrasive behavior before from a cop. You did not want a person like Trooper Freely to be, pissed off at you by any standard — on, or off duty for this matter.

I sat around longer, and thought about all sorts of things Freely might do next. My intuition told me to high tail this sucker outta here, and for a second I wondered deep down ... what if I am overreacting, and wrong about him. Maybe he is only going to run the registration, plates, etc., and discover my driver's license status is clean, and let me go free, or would he?

Something was not quite right with this whole picture though. I had the distinct feeling, that he could be conjuring up a far more sinister motive, and I did not want to stick around to find out.

When he began walking back to his cruiser with my license and proof of insurance, again my "mind" told me to leave. By doing so I would be able to prevent the possibility of an, "out of control conflict" with this maniac.

My body on the other hand said no, and every time I tried to place my foot on the gas pedal, some uncontrollable force prevented me from following through. The timing to leave was perfect, but instead I decided not to chance it. Therefore, I stood still and waited for his next move.

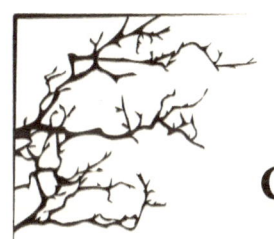

Chapter 10

The anxiety started to set in, and seemed as though an hour had passed by since Freely left. I figured if this psychopath is up to no good, he would've already tried to make his move. I began to perspire, my heart started skipping beats, and many thoughts crossed my mind. Thoughts such as...maybe there is a warrant out for my arrest, which I may be unaware of? Did I forgot to pay motor vehicle violations from years ago? Is he is taking long because he is waiting for the cavalry to show up to have back-up while placing me under arrest? Is he going to write me a ticket?

A million other things bombarded my brain as I thought of possible motives for why he took so long. For whatever reason, I felt compelled to peek behind me to catch a glimpse of him. The wait and stress of not knowing drove me crazy to the point where I needed to know. So I turned back to locate him, but to my surprise he was gone — "poof." Freely was nowhere in sight. It was if he had just vanished off the face of the earth.

I was rather pleased by this discovery. On the other hand, Freely's disappearance left me a bit puzzled, and concerned. That "little inner voice" told me something was not quite right, and my intuition caused me to take immediate action. I decided now would be a perfect opportunity to split.

So with my head turned towards Freely's vehicle, I wasted no time and slammed my foot down hard on the accelerator. Bad luck soon followed when the back tires spun out of control, causing me to be stuck in the mud. Not good I thought.

Now trapped and going nowhere, the panic sprang-up full force. To add to the fuel, in the background the voice of a police dispatcher began questioning Freely's whereabouts. She had tried to reach him on the radio for quite some time. This only made me more paranoid, and apprehensive.

Screw it, I thought. Without any disinclination, I let off on the gas... pushing back down on the pedal to rock the car forward, so I would grasp a little tread on the loosely pebbled graveled road. I began to push down harder, when she tried reaching Freely a fourth time with no success.

By now, I could not locate Freely anywhere, and to make matters worse, the heavy eerie fog outside made seeing anything unmanageable. What is going on here? I thought... is he arched over the front seat of his vehicle somewhere? I had no idea where he went. I wondered if maybe something bad had happened to him.

While the dispatcher waited for a reply back from Freely, a sound from his patrol car caught me off guard, and I could hear heavy breathing impending from inside his cruiser. Soon thereafter, came utter silence. Then more deep huffing sounds followed. The noise became louder somewhere from further up in the woods, not too far from near the trail.

As I looked over towards the direction in the field — off the trail leading to old man farmer Bill's place...was what I can only describe as being, "a thing from not of this earth." In the distance, sat a very tall thin looking shadow like figure of a young girl — not an ordinary one... mine you! In fact she creeped the hell out of me as she swung from a rope attached to a tree. At first, I thought she had not seen me, but as I continued to watch her from a distance, she turned her head toward me, stared straight at me, smiled, and then casually began rocking back and forth on the swing. This slender extraterrestrial looking thing showed up out of nowhere, and had my complete full attention. This child's awkward presence sent shivers down my spine.

While swinging from the rope, she held a portable radio in one of her long straggly hands. She placed the transmitter up close to her mouth, and responded to the police dispatcher who was still trying to contact Trooper Hank Freely. I could hear the dispatcher's voice muttering from both Freely's patrol cruiser, and from his portable which was now being held, and controlled by this very strange looking girl, who sat swinging near the trail.

"Freely what's your twenty — copy?" "Unit 32, please respond to dispatch via phone if your portable transmitter is not functioning," stated the 911 dispatcher.

The girl placed the radio transmitter closer to her mouth and responded to dispatch with an eerie like smile — followed by heavy puffs of breathing. She started to cackle into Freely's portable, and only a few seconds had transpired, before I realized what had happened.

No doubt, this creepy girl had something to do with Hanks disappearance. Here she is, (this god-forsaken damn freak of nature) now holding his police radio, and not one visual sign, or evidence of him anywhere. How very odd.

While I attempted to free the car's tires again from the slippery mud, I could still see her menacing smile from the corner of my eyes. Meanwhile, the grotesque looking abnormal sized girl continued staring. I tried to get my mind off this alien species, and Trooper Freely, but instead concentrated on executing my next move.

It was obvious I was going nowhere. I needed to think of an alternative plan, and quick. I still had not quite recalled the reason for being here in the first place. Only bits and pieces of distraught memory rattled in the brain. Everything seemed so fuzzy.

I told myself I was not awake yet from this terrible dream, and would eventually wake up from this whole ordeal and laugh this off later. When though, would I wake up from this horrific dream?

Soon I began to rationalize the reasoning behind all the confusion, pain, and recent memory loss, but the more I tried to put the puzzle together, the more confused I became. I started to laugh it off — mumbling aloud to myself:

"This is nothing other than a bad nightmare. That is all... only a figment of the imagination — the odd girl, Freely, and this trail. None of them really existed."

I started to laugh more, and got out of the car to approach the girl, who now had remained swinging and holding Freely's portable radio in her hands. As I inched my way closer, she began to giggle again, and seemed rather unfazed by my brash decision to confront her. In the back of my mind I assumed the police dispatcher had figured out a problem existed with Hank, and therefore already went ahead to send out a back-up unit to his location.

Feeling more confident now, I started taking abrupt baby steps towards her. Then I hesitated for a brief moment before approaching any further. I thought to myself... *after all, she is only a harmless freak. Even though she scares the bloody hell out of me, what harm could she really do?*

Now about ten feet away from her, I shouted:

"Hey...What are you doing out here?" There was no reply. She continued to stare me down with her psycho like snicker, and cracked another one of those morbid smiles. "Are you deaf girl?" "I'm talking to you," I yelled out.

When I looked over at the kid for some kind of reply, she started to get off the swing. I slowly backed away from her, about two feet or so, and then she raised her hand, and aimed one of her fingers out towards Hanks police cruiser. This odd behavior seemed familiar, but I couldn't recall why. Only when I decided to turn my head away from the girl to see what she pointed at, did I begin to have flashbacks regarding a dark shadowy figure who once before in the past, pointed out towards the lake while I stood in awe by myself smoking cigarettes back at the cabin.

I started to experience this whole scenery again, and I wondered if perhaps this was somehow connected to this figure outside my cottage, or was it even my cottage?

Suddenly, without any inclination, a sharp and unsettling sensation struck my entire body. The pain abruptly stopped — only lasting a few seconds or so, but felt much longer. What in the hell is this? I shook my head, and tried to gain back my composure. I peered out towards where Freely's cruiser had been parked, but his vehicle was now gone. He was still nowhere in sight. The trail disappeared, my car is no longer here, and the girl had vanished!

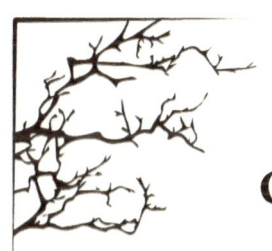

Chapter 11

In the background, I could now hear a soft feeble, but stern voice say, "9, 10,"

When I came to, my eyes began to focus in on a blinking light, and I saw a familiar face. His name is Dr. Albert Stern, and he is perhaps one of the most renowned Psychiatrist in the area. Dr. Stern is not just my doctor, but is also a good friend. I trusted him with my life, and he was trying to help bring back my recent memory loss through implementing and inducing a suggestive therapeutic process, known as "medical hypnotherapy."

In the past, Stern had attempted to use other various traditional counseling methodologies such as cognitive therapy, psychotherapy, Gestalt therapy, and even tried using an innovative system of approach called, coaching.

None of these quite worked, and for many of them the process took too long, and most of them were exceptionally tedious — all accept for one. The one exception was the power of hypnosis, which started working immediately. Through the powerful induction of this "clinical application," my memory came back a little at a time, or at least that is what I thought.

Stern began to go over the results from the hypnosis session and found my progress very similar to the previous week's hypnotherapy sessions. So as a result, he advocated doing an advanced stage of hypnosis. This, he yearned would get me into a more unperturbed state of consciousness, thus helping me dig deeper into the subconscious mind... to recall past events.

By this point, I became enthusiastic to try anything. The pain of not knowing about the past was painful enough. I knew that I had suffered from what Dr. Stern had referred to as, Post-Traumatic Stress Syndrome. This being the case, the good doctor prescribed medicine to both ease the suffering and to help focus better. The medical scripts would also aid in the overall procedure with "clinical hypnosis" by alleviating any added stress, thereby creating a more optimistic result.

Stern wanted to begin new hypnotherapy sessions right away, and had suggested to set up an appointment with his assistant later in the week. However, I also was anxious to start the process, and therefore was insistent in having him begin the treatments sometime the same day — perhaps even during the nighttime.

After he thought about it for a few minutes, he finally permitted to see me later in the evening. I went to make the appointment with Doc's secretary, and then made a quick departure out the door.

After arriving home, I set the cell phone alarm for six o'clock PM, positioned myself down in bed, looked up at the ceiling, and fell asleep.

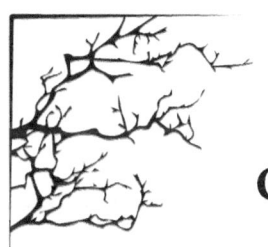

Chapter 12

L ater the same evening, I found myself back again in the good old doctor's office. Dr. Stern first checked all the vital signs, things like blood pressure, heart rate, and other various anatomic components. He put a CD on consisting of serene music melodies, and began the hypnosis process. He wanted me to concentrate on relaxing as much as possible. "I want you to be in a relaxed state before we begin," he said.

After about what seemed like fifteen minutes of this unwinding stage, my whole body became so dense that I practically could feel myself levitate off the ground. This procedure placed me in a very comfortable position. I was now in a complete state of well-being.

"Concentrate on visualizing yourself walking down a dark quiet stairwell. Stay relaxed and continue to focus on descending further and further down the stairs as I count backwards from 100," he said. I concentrated while he counted. By the time he reached 50, I had drifted off into a hypnotic state.

Then complete darkness overwhelmed me. Dr. Stern wanted to know what happened next. "Go on; tell me everything step by step — detail by detail of how it all began. This time reveal to me what actually happened," Stern said.

Stern's voice started to fade away, and I now found myself alone in the dark. I drifted further into my subconscious mind, and began to narrate my story in more detail — this time remembering everything as it happened.

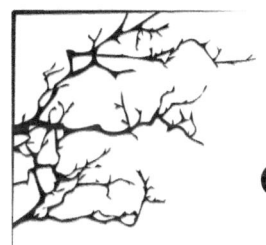

Chapter 13

Before long, I found myself inside a vehicle with several lifeguards from the lake. Right away I recognized one of the guards sitting down behind the steering wheel, and there driving a jeep wrangler sat, Bulldog.

I began to tell Dr. Stern what happened:

"Outside, darkness came on fast and the rain poured down from the gloomy gray sky. Water dripped from the branches above and pelted the windshield of bulldog's vehicle as we cruised up the mountainside. Bulldog and the others were in route — traveling a little further up the Adirondack Mountains region. Up in the isolated backwoods of the valley, lied Camp Little Rock. Bulldog drove in that direction. The campsite had been abandoned most of the year, but was now being used for a training facility to certify lifeguards."

"By the time we finally arrived at the campground, it was pitch dark outside. As we drove up to the site, several abandoned cabins laid spaciously spread out —shouldering one another — forming what looked like a spherical shape.

Inside the circle of cottages, a few old burnt logs lied on the ground from a previous campfire."

"Further in the distance, away from the cabins lied a heavily wooded trail that appeared to lead to the lake behind the campground. Near the entrance hung a big green rectangular sign that read, Old Man Farmer Bill's Trail. Below the trail's sign dangled a second smaller yellow one with red lettering warning hikers and campers of nearby bears, and other wild animals in the area."

"By the time we got settled inside our separate cabins, I felt exhausted. Therefore, I decided to retire for the evening to get an early morning start before our first lifeguard training session. I set my alarm, and immediately went outdoors to tell the others. Outside everyone huddled around a campfire talking and laughing. I told them good night, and proceeded to walk back to the cabin."

Still under hypnosis, I subconsciously heard Dr. Stern's faint voice, as he continued to probe me for further information.

"What happened next?" stated Dr. Stern. I paused for a few moments before proceeding to tell Dr. Stern the rest of the story:

"After reaching my cabin I laid down on the bed and then it happened. I had a hard time sleeping, so I proceed outdoors again to see what the others were up too, but upon arriving outside, I noticed everyone was gone. I looked around near the campfire, and out by the other cabins. I found no sign of anyone. They had all disappeared, and their fire still burned red hot embers."

"Apprehensive and more than a bit nervous now, I decided to have a smoke. I began to light my cigarette, when a noise coming from near the trail entrance startled me. The sound of what sounded of "grunt callings" rang out from the woods, along with weird ruffling sounds, like tree branches being stepped on. It became increasingly louder, and seemed to gain momentum, almost as if someone was closing in very fast. I prayed to God lifeguards would appear from out of the dark, but they didn't come out — something else did."

"Someone did pop out of the forest, only not who I projected. While I stood frozen from fear, waiting for the "mysterious unknown" to appear, a black fog, or mist sprang out into the open. This thing got closer and began to interchange slowly — almost hovering over the top of the ground. Moments later, in an instant, this eerie haze transformed, and shapeshifted itself into a human like creature, and crawled towards me making a blood-curdling howling sound."

"Now scared to death of its intention, I saw hands begin to spring out, as if in slow motion. Seconds later two anomalous looking feet stretched out into view, and then this unusual deformed creature hovered through the air only inches away from me."

"I noticed its long neck, and then a head pop out that moved back and forth, while turning side to side like a wild animal scanning the forest for its prey. I did not think it noticed me at first, but suddenly this thing started crawling towards me. I made sure to never take all eyes off it as I tried to retreat to the cabin. I began slowly inching closer to the cottage when a sharp noise echoed out from the still darkness — piercing my ears."

"Following this intense deafening sound, a bright-bluish light blinded me, and the heat from this intense illumination started to burn my body from the inside out. Now on fire, the pain became unbearable. I squawked out loud pleading, praying, and hoping to die fast so this nightmare would subside."

"After what seemed like one hour had passed, the rays and heat from this beam expired out, and shortly thereafter the suffering wholly diminished, as if nothing ensued, almost as though I had been dreaming."

"A few minutes after these chain of events took place, did I get a better depiction of this strange phenomenon transform into something inhuman like. This thing had, "creature feature," qualities you found in any unnerving horror movie. The creature stood up screaming — brandishing blood dripping canine teeth, and slanted ears stretching far out away from its head. Its skin and forehead appeared abnormal, and so were its feet and hands. For some unknown reason, its long skeleton shaped fingers pointed in the direction — off towards the lake."

"I wanted to look to the water but a force from the tortuous ray of light earlier (which resembled a magnet) began to drag and pull me — sucking me further and deeper in. Inside this beam and in the distance I saw what looked like some kind of "red glowing door" surrounded by darkness. Panicky, I was hesitant to proceed any further, but all that changed when something nudged me from behind, causing me to approach even closer."

"Moments later the prevailing force from the beam of light pulled me directly in front of this "glowing spectacle." The door appeared only partially open. I became skeptical and somewhat reluctant to walk in, and decided not to enter at all.

Not long thereafter, something began grouping my legs and pushed me further along through the entrance. I hadn't noticed the hands at first, but when I got a quick glimpse of them, they appeared to be webbed-like and silver in color."

"Heavy breathing sensations smothered my face and legs and entire body, while more than several of these things began to surround me. I did not see their bodies, nor did I really want too.

My eyes stayed closed, wishing for the whole experience to evaporate, but it did not end. I had the distinct feeling this was only the beginning of a never ending episode for which would continue forever; and what befell next was something not from this planet — not from this world."

Dr. Stern's voice continued to guide me: "OK good. Now concentrate, stay focused and explain the meaning of, "not from this world." Give all the details. Go on, what happened next?"

By this point into the hypnosis session, recollecting everything from then on was grim. Trying to recall the events as they occurred one after the other had been especially hard. For reasons unknown, most of the imperative details of my memory were erased, deleted — wiped out.

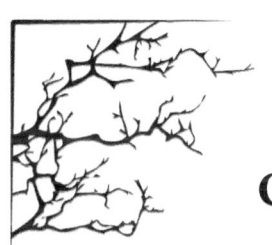

Chapter 14

Many of the events of what happened during this night remained fuzzy and blurry. I recalled how Dr. Stern mentioned to me (before beginning our hypnosis session) that trying to bring back my memory may be very painful. In fact, he said I most likely "obliterated" everything from my mind so I would forget all these negative memories. I wanted to remember though. I had to put this insane puzzle together, and did not want to feel this way anymore. I hated not knowing, and prayed for closure. I needed my life restored.

Think, concentrate, I told myself. I focused on what happened next, and I soon went back to the place where I left off with Dr. Stern, but I no longer had those creepy hands scrabbling all over me. Now, only complete darkness shadowed, and before long, I recalled the next set of events:

"I remember shivering (in the middle of summer) from being cold while walking slowly outside in the pitch black (for what seemed like a half a mile) trying to find some light and heat. Petrified at this point, I panicked and started yelling aloud — only listening to my own frightened voice echo back at me. In denial, I waited for a while before realizing these anxious screams for help were going unnoticed."

"Where am I? Maybe I'm imprisoned inside some bizarre tunnel, which leads to eternal hell I thought. Shortly afterwards, something else happened. My entire body became constricted, and I no longer could budge. I tried to move both hands and legs, but the only part, which would shift freely — side to side, was my eyes. During this time, I did not see or hear anything, and everything remained pitch black."

"The calm stillness of the eerie darkness was shattered when morbid sounds of terror broke the silence. I did not know where the screeches came from. I could hear them though, plain as day. Only I wished I hadn't. I wanted so bad to block the horrifying sounds from traveling to my ears, but I could not, because both my hands would not break free."

"These noises had been the obvious shrieks of torture. The high-pitched screams had been so horrific, and I was unable to tell if they came from women, men, or if the blood curdling screaming had even been mortal. Then they stopped. For a minute, it became quiet, until I felt heavy breathing on my body. I kept rolling my eyes back and forth (the only part of me which moved) — hoping and praying I would not be next. I wanted to scream, but my mouth had been glued shut with something. I tried one more time to escape from the restraints, only this idea proved to be useless. I was trapped."

"What is going to happen to me? What is happening here? I thought about this for a few more seconds, when teeth chatter noises came from near my face. The chattering would last for only a moment, stop and continue some more, ended, and then start up again."

"Suddenly, the sounds abruptly stopped, a dim light flicked on, and I saw strange eyes staring back at me. Several other brighter lights flickered on from the far corner of the room. They shined down from the top of the ceiling, directly down on what appeared to be operating counters covered with white, bloodstained bedspreads. Human legs and arms stuck out from underneath the blood soaked sheets. In the next cot to the left, Bulldog lied there over in the distance — lifeless, and not moving."

"My eyes wandered off scanning for the remaining inhabitants in the room. I presumed the several bodies on these operating beds, which surrounded this place, might perhaps be... my other missing lifeguard friends, and other 'unfortunates' reported missing throughout the years."

"In one corner appeared to be what looked like Trooper Freely lying next to Corporal Zimmerman and his wife. Freely tried to move, but he too was immobilized down to his bed."

"In the other far end lied "old man farmer Bill." None of them moved, and numerous blood saturated sheets concealed various parts of their bodies."

"While I laid helpless awaiting my fate, I couldn't help marvel what might become of me, or why any of this had come to pass in the first place. I thought about Bill and how he yakked of witnessing these odd-looking little people with pitchforks, seen neighboring the trail leading to his farmstead. Maybe he had been right after all. Nevertheless, I was more than convinced I would find out for certain, if what he spoke about was factual."

"By now, my heart began hammering out of my chest, and I had felt the perspiration consume my body. I could not spot my assailants anywhere. All I detected were these bloody — battered up bodies."

"After a few moments, a little boy came out of nowhere wearing a half covered white gurney, and he started to approach my bed. He appeared normal and acquitted enough, and for an ephemeral moment, I wondered if he too was detained against his will."

"Then the miniscule boy ambled up, and there in his hands was bulldogs multi-colored whistles. He seemed captivated by them as he inquisitively began to play with each separate one — like some sort of toy. After what seemed like a thorough inspection of each one of the whistles, he started to blow into them — one at a time. The boy continued to puff away!"

"After he finished playing he giggled, smiled, looked over at me, and began to chatter his teeth together. Then the lights went dark, and I overheard what sounded like the scuffling of feet close in on me. Now they had been essentially on top of me. In the background the others began screaming."

The first shrill of pain came from inside my nostrils, as they abducted me, using sharp protracting needles. Their experimentation continued, and soon after, I could feel excruciating discomfort down around the intermediate area of my spine. Before long, they were trying to in-lodge an object into the frontal lobe portion of my brain.

Soon, the sound of a skull being crushed rang out, as the drill ripped through flesh which created a gush of blood that splattered all over the side of my face." After the drilling stopped Stern spoke again, "what happened next?"

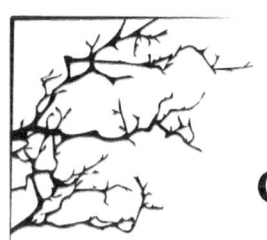

Chapter 15

Still under suggestive hypnosis, I tried to recall the next set of circumstances, which took place after the abduction. I told Dr. Stern I remembered following old man farmer Bill into the woods, and about the unusual run-in with Freely out in front of the trail, along with the eccentric slender girl. Somehow, though I seemed to have forgotten everything after this, including what really went on during the search for Bill, or why I had even followed him in the first place! Everything before, and after these chain of events remained a blur, as if my memory had been wiped out!

Dr. Stern's voice reverberated throughout the hypnosis session, and again he commenced to ask more information:

"What happened after you came back from the woods? Try hard and think about everything which took place regarding trooper Freely, and the outlandish slender girl that night upon your return."

The subconscious mind went to work again, as I tried to recollect all the specific events and how they unfolded during this time. With both eyes still barred, I hesitated for a moment before answering Stern:

"Oh my God, I yelled." "What?"... Stern said.

With a sneer on my face, I replied to Stern: "I remember everything now."

"Good, now we're getting somewhere. Go on, tell me," Dr. Stern said.

"Wow, I understand now. Somehow, I think I have solved the puzzle... I know what it all means, and who I really am," I shouted.

"What and who are you?" Stern asked:

"I recall everything that happened to me... Freely, and old man farmer Bill that night,"

For a moment, my eyes remained closed shut under fluttering eyelids, until something caused me to fling them wide open. This sudden awakening took both Stern and I by surprise. Still in a hypnotic trance, and lying down on Dr. Sterns couch, I sprang my body into an upright position — like a hungry desperate vampire waking up from his coffin. Stern, a bit taken aback asked, "what happened to you... what?"

I locked my eyes onto Stern's, smiled at him and said: "After I was abducted by these things, I became one of them, and began shapeshifting, and stalking everybody in town. God, I cannot believe this. I remember helping to abduct lots of them, but at the time, I had not been aware of it!

"Oh come on me dear young lady, this is preposterous," Stern replied.

I turned my head towards Stern, as if possessed by demons. Standing behind

Dr. Stern's desk stood a tall wide mirror, and I could only see his reflection, but not mine.

In utter astonishment, I lifted my finger, and pointed straight at the mirror. Curious, Stern shifted his entire body back to look, and said, "Oh my God." Then Dr. Stern turned his head back at me and screamed!

Acknowledgements:

I wish to first thank all my family members who have continuously been there for me. Without all their support, I probably would not be here. I wish to thank my wife, Gloria Mentillo for all her love, patience, support, and comments of advice which by the way, I should have listened to sooner.

The same holds true for my brother, Jeremy Mentillo who also happens to be my best friend. However, due to being so damn humble, he will never admit that without his professional input as a decorated State Trooper, and Investigator involving editing, along with his endless knowledge of true crime and the macabre, I would have never succeeded. Ya brother, you heard me!

I also wish to thank my mother, Marie Mentillo who also happens to be the best mother in the world. Without all your support, none of these projects would have life. You truly are a mother every son should have. I also would like to truly thank my father, Robert Mentillo for "always believing in me," but more importantly teaching me to believe in myself. Your steadfast commitment of encouragement and wisdom are why I keep on keeping on.

I wish to thank my sister, Mellissa Mentillo who happens to be my main inspiration for writing. Remember when we were kids, and all those very long hours of reading, "The Hardy Boys, and Nancy Drew stories together?" Well, that is how it all really began. You taught me how to read hundreds of books in one summer. You truly opened me up to the world of books in general.

Additionally, I wish to thank horror writer, "Stephen King" for giving me inspiration to never quit writing. Thank you for all your knowledge and wisdom. A true leader helps others succeed. You have always shared (through open arms) what you have learned as a writer to others. Thank you for that. You truly are, a "King."

Finally, I want to sincerely thank all those who have purchased this book, and my previous books. Obviously, without you people, I would not have the means for which to write and share my stories with. You are truly awesome.

About The Author:

C **hris Mentillo Ph.D.,** aka, "Doc Mentillo" was born in Auburn, New York. He grew up in Skaneateles, New York and later moved to the Boston, Massachusetts New England Area, where he finished receiving his formal education.

During his tenure in New England, he began writing about his real-life spiritual and paranormal experiences while documenting them in his personal journal. These unusual, "true occurrences" recorded, were used in his previous radio show broadcasts. This later lead to him writing about true crime mixed with horror and the supernatural for which he believes all intertwine.

Additionally, he has written movie scripts, songs, and books, which usually fall into the supernatural horror genre or the Macabre.

Other Authors such as H. P. Lovecraft, Stephen King, and Edgar Allan Poe also used similar macabre atmosphere in their works.

Dr. Chris Mentillo holds a degree from Bradford College, in Haverhill Massachusetts. He is also a graduate of, The Criminal Justice Training Council Institute from Northeastern University's Ph.D. Program, and Deaconess Hospital, Longwood Medical Center's Doctorate program (Palmer 5

Building) involving, clinical medical hypnotherapy, and criminal psychology located in Boston, Massachusetts. He currently resides in Massachusetts with his wife, Gloria.

Don't miss out!

Visit the website below and you can sign up to receive emails whenever Chris Mentillo publishes a new book. There's no charge and no obligation.

https://books2read.com/r/B-A-PATC-WYWJ

BOOKS 2 READ

Connecting independent readers to independent writers.

Also by Chris Mentillo

Obliterated: Everything is About To Change

Watch for more at https://HorrorPublishing.com.

About the Author

Award-winning, and best-selling horror author, Chris Mentillo recounts bone-chilling horror tales of, first-hand weird and bizarre encounters. Confronted repeatedly by ghastly, disturbing dreams, monstrous shadows of things to become, and many more frightening events, Chris Mentillo is changed forever when brought back into real-life events, only to find himself experiencing the horrors of what came to pass of people's deaths.

Sometimes driven there to stop a horrific event from taking place, or there for other unknown reasons. Nevertheless, the horrors never seize to end from deep inside these pictures of real nightmares.

Now for the very first time ever, never published: *Nightmares of A Horror Author – Beyond Dreams; chronicles* the true stories of a horror author's terrifying encounters with the dark side. Obliterated, "Everything is About to Change" is part of these thrilling events.

Read more at https://HorrorPublishing.com.

About the Publisher

Horror Press Publishing -- is an *award-winning*, professional horror publishing imprint, based out of Boston, Massachusetts.

Originally, it was developed solely as a print label to promote various horror books. However, the *publishing imprint* is now involved with more than just horror books. The label currently concentrates on formulating and creating anything, and everything horror related within the entertainment, and publishing industry, etc.

The imprints original founding member was pulp-fiction, best-selling, science-fiction author and producer, of the popular television series...*The Twilight Zone, Rod Serling.* The imprint's current owner now is, *Gloria Pasztor.*

www.ingramcontent.com/pod-product-compliance
Lightning Source LLC
Chambersburg PA
CBHW020755130626
46554CB00006B/2192